About the author

J.D. Maguire is a novelist, scriptwriter and short story writer. He lives in Cambuslang, Glasgow, and works as a teacher of English at Bellshill Academy, where he runs an adult creative writing class.

GRÀDH AND OTHER SHORT STORIES

J.D. Maguire

GRÀDH AND OTHER SHORT STORIES

Vanguard Press

VANGUARD PAPERBACK

A CIP catalogue record for this title is available from the British Library.

ISBN 978 1 78465 801 4

Vanguard Press is an imprint of
Pegasus Elliot MacKenzie Publishers Ltd.
www.pegasuspublishers.com

First Published in 2020

Vanguard Press
Sheraton House Castle Park
Cambridge England

Printed & Bound in Great Britain

Dedication

Love to Eileen, Jack, David, Kevin, Yvonne, Megan, Maureen, Jose, John

And Kathleen.

Thanks to Marion Mitchell & Jacqueline Stewart.

Contents

Gràdh

Illustration by Jacqueline Stewart.

"Is it big?"

"Even bigger than the carriage clock potato."

Bleary-eyed, he stared at the wall-mounted forty-inch plasma television screen while biting into his cold toast. Standing, he allowed his middle-age spread to comfortably rest on the back of the two-seat sofa, as he hypnotically watched Sky News reporter Justin Meade and a scrum of other good men and ladies of the press chase the MP for East Deckart all the way up his garden path, before he finally escaped beyond the 'his and her' Range Rover TDV8s in the driveway and inside his reluctant front door! Mr Family Values: done and pretty much dusted. The other woman hadn't even been 'outed' yet: but a result is a result. He grinned as he watched a smug Meade – who had broken the story late last night – look into the camera lens and pontificate to a grateful nation. *You bastard*, he thought. *You lucky bastard!*

He always stopped in the same place. The road into Gràdh had a steep gradient, spiralling forever downward, it seemed. At this lay-by he could see the whole village and surrounding area. *Welcome to Gràdh*, whispered the sign. *Population: 220.*

Twinned with Village Modèle. It was the last piece of information that always made him grin: *The Second Smallest Village in Scotland!* Typical! Surely even the keenest of wayward Americans would immediately swing the car around at this 'news' and go in search of number one!

He was interrupted by the purring of a shiny Mercedes travelling upwards that had pulled in alongside his grey Punto.

"Ian Moyes grown another cabbage that looks like Michael Jackson?"

"It's bigger than that. And it was a cauliflower. And it was Stevie Wonder."

"Surely not another potato carriage clock?"

"Bigger!"

"Bigger? Wow!"

"Yip. Carol Ann Love, twenty-five years…"

"I don't think I'll be able to contain myself until next week. Bye!"

With that, the car shot out of the small lay-by carrying his ex-wife on her journey upwards. As he looked after her for a few seconds and then turned and looked down the way, towards his destination, he couldn't help but think what a nice little metaphorical microcosm of his life had just been played out.

As he drove along Gràdh's main street, David Tait had to admit just how picturesque the village really looked – particularly on fresh, spring days like this. The cottages and their spacious flower-filled lawns looked as if they could've been captured by Thomas Kinkade. He slowed down as he neared the end of the buildings, though the road continued onward to several more shades of green and yellow pastures. Pulling into the driveway of the last building on the left-hand side, he admired the modern façade of the Library. Two-storied. A mixture of gleaming oak surround and tinted glass. It had once been his favourite place to study, to research, to hide. When similar facilities had closed, when the cost to stay open had become too prohibitive, this building had somehow thrived. When he was very young, Vera Love had been the librarian. She had continued to be so, long after he had moved out. Then one day he heard that she was dead and, almost immediately, her daughter Carol Ann had stepped in to fill her shoes. And here we were – twenty-five years later.

It really was a case of 'out with the old', because the place was immediately transformed: computers, furniture, coffee room on the second floor at the rear, overlooking Gràdh's forty shades of green. The village didn't grow population-wise in any significant way, so David Tait could only tip his metaphorical cap towards Ms Love's unique formula – whatever it was – that had allowed her 'business' to thrive while similar facilities failed. In fact, he would have congratulated her immediately but for a rather major problem. The front door entrance was locked.

Again, Tait tried the handle. Nothing. He peered through the glass door, then the rest of the tinted glass as he made his way around the building, looking for any sign of life. Finally, he reached the rear and the emergency exit. Nothing amiss. He hoped by the time he had made his way back around to the front of the library, Carol Ann Love would have arrived. He held up his hands to protect his eyes from the low sun and he surveyed the road to his left, then his right. Nothing. No one. However, a glance at the watch on his right wrist revealed there was some good news: 11.04. Pub's open!

He again looked around about the front of the library, as if Ms Love was about to suddenly materialise, and then – maybe even more ridiculously – he tried the front door again. He sighed loudly and, as if imagining an audience, he shook his head. Then, with some sort of decision-making process in operation, he took one last look at his watch before heading out of the library car park and veering right.

He strolled past the beautifully manicured lawns for five minutes or so before turning to face *The Village*. It was set back fifty feet or so from the road and had a dozen wooden tables with accompanying benches outside. The pub, with its white sandstone and ornate hanging baskets, smiled cheerfully back at him. Tait checked for traffic either way, which made him laugh inside as – since entering Gràdh twenty-odd minutes or so ago – he hadn't seen a car or indeed any…

Suddenly, the door of *The Village* exploded open and Farmer Moyes burst out, turned sharply to his right and began heading in the direction of his farmland, his giant strides greedily eating up the yards in front of him.

Tait called out, "All right, Ian?"

As he watched Moyes disappear at great speed into the distance without any sort of recognition towards him, Tait pondered for a few seconds that it was just this sort of investigative and insightful questioning that had seen him become Chief Reporter of the *Gràdh and Pleasant Post*. And Editor. And Photographer. And Headline Writer. And… well, I could go on, he thought, but one thing he had uncovered moments ago – the pub was most definitely open!

Pushing open the heavy oak door, he was greeted with the sight of a fantasy figure from his youth: Sheila Munn. Later, she had made it clear she had designs on him. By then, he was more than just uninterested – he was shocked. And disgusted. She had inherited *The Village* from her dead husband. Poor Frank. He had died in his early thirties – falling down some stairs – leaving her to look after a pub and four young children. Tait had always admired her for not folding; for not giving in. It couldn't have been easy. Yet she seemed to thrive. She had never married again. All the kids had done well, moving first to university, then good, secure employment. Kevin – the middle lad – had eventually gone into the licensing trade and now had a string of bars stretching from Pleasant to East Deckart and beyond. *The Village* wasn't one of them, though. It remained independent. In tribute to his dad – and especially his mum. As a loving son, though, he made sure Sheila never lacked support: always helping with staffing and indeed cashflow during the quiet winter months when visitors to the village were at a premium.

"Bloody hell, you're early."

"Hey, it's five o'clock somewhere. Besides, I see I'm not your first customer."

"Eh? Oh, Ian. He doesn't count. Not really."

"Why's that?"

"'Cause he's just part of the furniture now at this time."

"It's not doing a lot for him. He didn't even look in my direction. A double…"

"Jack Daniels and ice?"

"You remembered."

"How could I forget?"

Sheila excused herself for a few minutes and went into the kitchen to discuss the lunchtime menu with “her chef”. Tait looked around the old place, full of many happy memories. He was just finishing his drink when Sheila returned.

Placing his empty glass on top of the bar, he asked, “So, what’s up with Ian anyway?”

“Oh, God knows. He’s been like that for about a month. You know what he’s normally like: very even-keeled. Never up nor down. Just Ian. He always takes everything in his stride. But ever since the Poetry Club meeting…”

“Whoa! Gràdh’s got a Poetry Club?”

“I’m gonna ignore the sarcasm in your voice, Mr Tait. They meet once a fortnight and I can tell you from personal experience that it’s very good fun. And educational.”

With great effort, Tait resisted the urge to make a smart-ass comment about this oxymoron.

The conversation continued as Tait walked across the floor to the exit. He was just about to leave, after being unable to stop himself from commenting that the club couldn’t be particularly beneficial considering that Sheila couldn’t remember the name of the “Scottish Woman” whose poem the group had last “looked at” and the mood that Moyes had been in when he had left.

Sheila faked annoyance and said, “Well, we enjoy it. So did Ian. Right up until two meetings ago anyway. He had a face like thunder when they came in.”

"They?"

"Yeah. We always start dead on eight, but this time we were one short. It was so unusual; everyone is always so punctual. Ian, always the gentleman, volunteered to do the 'round-up'. He was as cheery as ever when he left, but his mood changed completely in the two minutes he'd been outside."

"Who had he gone to get?"

"Funny now. Kept muttering about 'Gas Guzzlers', 'Flash Git', 'Bloody Townies in their 4x4s'."

"Who?"

"He never said."

"No. Who had he fetched?"

Hearing the answer, Tait hesitated in the glare of the late morning sun. Then he turned around and went back inside.

"Double JD with ice?"

***

It was after mid-day and he was again standing in front of the library building. This time he had been joined by two of the local worthies – probably husband and wife. They were concerned. The library was never closed.

"Not during opening time anyway," the woman explained.

Something must be wrong. Carol Ann was always very punctual. *Most times*, Tait thought. As they made their way back along the road, they stopped, turned and looked at the building itself, as if it could provide an answer for them.

Tait – in his modest little grey Punto – made his way back out onto the Main Road and past *The Village*. About a hundred yards or so later, he turned into Braebank Way. As he did so, the red Mercedes from earlier sped past him in the opposite direction. The Way curved to the right and ran – for a short distance – parallel to the Main Street. Of the two houses in this quiet cul-de-sac, Carol Ann Love's was the second. Beyond it, behind a thick grouping of trees, was a makeshift car park which in turn led to more forest, and beyond, some of the most spectacular views of this green land and surrounding areas.

Pulling in next to Love's gleaming white picket fence, Tait again paused for a few seconds to admire the tranquillity of the beautiful, rural setting. When he emerged from his car, he was still enjoying the colours and the reassuring smell of newly cut grass. He stood outside the *Chocolate Box* cottage for a few seconds before moving towards the gate. He had just lifted the latch when he was disturbed by a roaring engine approaching from the same direction from which he had just come. Seconds later, Ian Moyes' jeep was speeding past him, before twisting dangerously beyond the group of trees and screeching to a halt at the edge of the woods. By the time Tait followed on foot, Moyes had 'parked', switched off the engine, slammed his door shut and was now, rapidly, disappearing into the woods. As Tait followed him – already a considerable distance behind – he noticed another vehicle partially obscured by Moyes' jeep.

A police patrol car.

As he ran through the wooded area, Tait occasionally lost sight of Moyes, his green jacket blending in with the surroundings. Ridiculously, he was no longer thinking that something serious must be going on up ahead, but instead was resolving – again – to lose some weight. The blood was pounding in his head and as he crossed a short wooden bridge over a small stream, he was forced to stop to catch his breath. As he did so, he looked through the gap to his right and saw the backs of two yellow-jacketed police officers staring straight ahead into a cluster of trees. Transfixed. Suddenly, they spun around in unison. Four hands were raised to stop the approaching two men and a German Shepherd who had just come into Tait's view. They needn't have worried. Moyes and another man had come to a halt and were mimicking the officers' previous stance. Only the dog wished to have a closer inspection, but it was gripped tightly by the second man. Tait heard distant sirens. Then close sirens. Then cars screeching to a halt. He moved a few feet to his left and then he stood. Transfixed. At the body. In the distance. The limp body. Hanging from a tree.

"Who is it?"

He turned, startled, and looked at his ex-wife. Behind her he could see four male uniformed police officers approach and another man dressed in a brown sports jacket, white shirt and pink tie. The group was moving briskly, but there was no rush. They already knew what was waiting for them just a few hundred yards down the slope to the right.

The man with the pink tie spoke. "Mornin'. We've got a serious incident here, as you've probably guessed. So I want you to go back up the path and outside the cordon."

The ashen-faced Tait nodded and began walking away. His ex-wife was beside him.

"Who is it?"

Tait continued walking, still stunned. They reached the end of the woods and saw more police officers. One female officer, dressed in an all-in-one white suit, lifted the tape which was stretched tightly between two trees at either end of the forest's entrance. She and two similarly dressed male colleagues ducked underneath and she continued holding as both Tait and his ex-wife crouched under. She nodded to them both, then turned and followed her fellow officers into the green wall.

***

Tait left the parking area still with his persistent companion in tow. He was walking quickly now. He arrived at his car, but fatally stopped for a few seconds and looked back at Love's cottage. Too late. The horse had bolted. The opportunity seized upon.

"Oh my god – Carol Ann!"

With those words, she spun around and headed for the gate of the cottage. He caught up with her, but not before she had pushed on the handle of the front door. Locked. She again turned quickly, pushing past Tait and heading around the side of the house towards the back. He caught up with her and gripped her arm tightly.

"What the hell are you doing?"

"For god's sake. You're the reporter. There's a *story* inside this house."

She stared defiantly at him for a few seconds, then pulled her arm away and carried on walking. He followed, and within seconds they were at a glass door. She reached for the white handle and pushed down. She froze as if she was a master criminal deep within some heavily fortressed bank vault, deciphering the safe code. Slowly. Respectfully. She eased open the door.

Tait followed her through to the rectangular-shaped kitchen. There was nothing on display at all save a clean, upright, empty coffee mug which had a picture of a perplexed-looking vicar and a parrot on it. Tait left the neat kitchen and went through to a small living room. Again, everything neat. Nothing disturbed. Leaving by the door on the other side of the room, he entered a short hallway. At its end he saw the locked front door and a staircase, on the left, leading upwards. There was another wooden door to his right. Despite it having a round doorknob, Tait was able to ease it open by putting his hand firmly against it.

Inside, it was the same again: clean, neat, tidy. He couldn't help but be impressed by Ms Love's cleaning habits. So impressed. Especially as she had obviously tidied up on what she must surely have known was her last night on this earth! He had wandered over to the marble fireplace, but there wasn't even as much as a circular or a bill in sight. Unless last night had been normal? Maybe this morning had brought something – something bad – to her door? He was just about to retreat back into the hall when he noticed that there were some leaflets or cards sitting flat on top of a small table by the bay window.

For some reason – maybe he felt some sort of nagging instinct that this was some kind of 'find' – he edged slowly across to the table. For what seemed like an age, but was probably only seconds, he stared down at the table top. He couldn't remember ever having being shocked too much in his life: not when his parents died; not when his wife left him. But now? Well, this was twice in a matter of minutes.

Suddenly, she was behind him again. "Is it big?"

"Even bigger than the carriage clock potato."

She came alongside him and looked at the photographs carefully laid out: on display. She stared at them and let out a short gasp of genuine surprise. Pictures of a man and one – one – of a smiling couple. She was holding the camera so both of the bright, beaming faces were close to the lens. Both of the unmistakeable faces; both of the recognisable faces: Carol Ann Love and Thomas Lord – MP for East Deckert.

"God, this is huge, so unbelievably huge. Jesus…"

"Yeah," was all Tait could muster.

"No one… no one knows who the 'other' woman is yet! This'll make you."

"Your friend, your friend from school, your friend from childhood, your friend from all of your years in this village, on this earth, died about half an hour ago!"

"And? She's not coming back. This is gonna catapult you into the Big Time. The chance to be a *real* reporter. The shot you've been waiting for all your life. It's here. Now take it."

She saw him staring back at her.

"What?"

"Listen to you. I'm almost fifty. There is no shot. Your friend…"

"Is dead! I know, I know. She's gone. The story…

"There is a story. Your friend has killed herself. That's it. A tragic story."

"The photographs are the *real* story."

"Yeah, a great story, eh? A great story to read. How your friend – *your* friend – after years of loneliness, fell in love with the *wrong* man. Isn't it enough she's dead? Isn't it enough that another family are suffering today, too? Where do you want this to end?"

"Print it. Print the story. Print the whole story!"

"Without the photographs there is no story. Not the type you mean."

"Print it and I'll come back. I'll come back. To you."

Tait was now staring back at her. He was adamant he hadn't misheard; he just couldn't quite comprehend what was being said.

"I mean it. I've climbed as high as I want to go. I don't want to go to London. I'll settle for being top dog around here. Top dogs. You and me. I'm bored. I know you taught him everything he knows. He knows it. He wants to keep flying. Not me. Not any longer!"

"Can you remember the rumours when your dad died? Can you remember what your own brother accused you of? Can you remember how you used to cry because Kevin wouldn't speak to you?"

"That was…"

"Destroy them. Destroy the photographs!"

He then spun around and headed towards the drawers of a glass display cabinet. Nothing. He made his way back into the living room, where there were two tables, each with a single drawer. Nothing. Going through a further set of drawers in the kitchen, he was beginning to despair. On reaching the fourth of five drawers, however… success. He hurriedly switched on the digital camera, turned to the photo display section and began to delete seven of the photographs saved there. After carefully replacing the camera, he slowly slid the drawer back into place.

His ex-wife was next to him again. She held up her right hand towards him, full of torn pieces of photographs. He took them from her, but walked past her, back to the front room.

"Don't trust me?"

He didn't answer; he just continued on his way. When he entered the room, he walked immediately over to the table. Satisfied there were no photographs lying on the table, or anywhere else that he could see, he turned and made his way to the back door. She was waiting for him.

"Satisfied?"

Again he didn't answer, but ushered her outside, before carefully shutting the door. They walked around to the front of the house and he wondered how long it would be before the police followed in their footsteps. They had just about reached their cars when Tait became aware of two men and a dog standing next to the trees, facing in the opposite direction, on the outskirts of the now busy 'parking' area. He was now able to make out that the man with the dog was Bobby Burns – newsagent and friend of Ian Moyes. Ian Moyes – huge, strong Ian Moyes – looked suddenly smaller. He was stooped and looked as if all the air had been knocked out of him. His grief for his friend – overwhelming. As sad a sight as it was, it had no effect on Tait. He had already decided to do what someone must.

His ex-wife now stood at the side of the shiny, red Mercedes. She had pulled open both the right front and rear doors. As he approached, however, she pushed the rear door closed again and then turned to face him.

"It's for the best, you know. No photos – no big story!"

She nodded. He then slipped his arms around her and held her tight against him for several seconds.

"Let me know of any funeral details? Good. Now take care."

What a day! You never knew what life was going to throw at you. Only a few hours earlier he'd approached Gràdh the same way he had before – hundreds of times. Now he was leaving and he couldn't quite grasp all that had happened: the suicide of a popular librarian; a completion of the circle of a sex scandal that had rocked Westminster – and his nearby town; and – perhaps the most surprising of all – his ex-wife offering to come back to him. Offering, or prostituting herself, he wondered?

As he drove up the sharp incline from the village, he pulled over into the lay-by he had stopped at earlier in the day. He got out and surveyed the scene below. He wondered when his birthplace, the perfect chocolate box scene, had transformed itself, magically, into such a centre of scandal. Maybe it had always been that way. Maybe as a child he hadn't noticed. Already indications of a fine investigative journalistic career ahead: always a great 'nose' for a story. He laughed out loud at just how useless he really was.

He felt inside his jacket pocket and pulled out a cigar. Given to him four months previously by the proud winner of January's Painting Pensioner, it had lain there ever since. From his right jacket pocket he took out his father's old lighter. Despite not smoking, he always carried it as a reminder: of someone good. He lit the cigar with more than a little difficulty. Leaning back against the body of his Punto, he puffed as expertly as he was capable. He heard a car approach from his right, then slow down, until it had stopped behind him.

"Celebrating?"

"Only my salvation – for what it's worth."

"Yeah? Good for you. A big story breaking, I believe?"

"A tragic one maybe. Local librarian's taken her life. But I guess you already know that, Mr Meade."

"Terrible, but more interested in the bigger picture. You know the one that links her with the local MP?"

"There's no story there. Not without photographs anyway. Just some tawdry rumours. The likes of Ian Moyes would kill you – and happily go to prison – if you besmirched an old friend with absolutely no proof."

"Just as well I've got proof, then. I think my darling wife may have *forgotten* to tear up one of the photographs in Love's house. Oops!"

"You know, Justin, if today has proved one thing, it's that you and Samantha belong together."

"Then I guess we're all happy?"

"Not really. A lot of people are miserable today."

"Well, what can you do?"

Meade's side window began to rise, but Tait motioned to him that their conversation was not quite at an end.

"Please tell my ex-wife, I really enjoyed holding her tight today. Although I think she already knows that."

Meade looked more puzzled than angry or jealous and gave a suspicious half-hearted laugh, before closing his window and speeding off into the distance. Tait watched him disappear, before walking around his car again. He made a furious effort to keep his cigar smoking, but finally gave up and tossed it into the greenery behind the small wall. He felt towards his inside pocket again, but this time produced a single photograph. He looked again at the couple's smiling faces – particularly Love's – before igniting his lighter once again and holding the bright flame to the photograph. He sighed, then got into his car and started the engine. He could be in Pleasant in three-quarters of an hour.

Then, and only then, he could begin the exposé of the 47 bus re-routing scandal that was the talk of… oh, at least fourteen people!

A Christmas Tale

Illustrations by Jacqueline Stewart

Molly looked at the winter's scene from her bedside window. Snow had been falling for two days now. Everywhere she looked seemed to be covered in huge swathes of white candyfloss. She giggled as she watched the huge inflatable Santa Claus across in the Talbots' front garden. He was rocking gently back and forth and every time he got towards the upright position it appeared that his outstretched hand was waving up at her. This Santa was Mr Talbot's centrepiece. His house was covered with… well, everything: flashing neon signs in the window, coloured lights around the top and bottom of his walls and – topping it all off – dazzling white lights which ran in a multitude of parallel lines from the roof to the ground. Molly gazed at the scene and noted her own personal favourite – the luminous Santa being pulled by his reindeer diagonally across the roof, as if about to take-off. Almost every house in the street – if not quite as 'attractively' as the Talbots' – was decorated. Almost every one. Molly felt mesmerised by so many colours painted against this giant white canvas. It was hard, but she pulled away from her bedroom window and turned inwards, towards her neat, clean, but decidedly bare room.

Having left her bedroom, Molly passed the closed door of another room and headed downstairs. She was aware of the slight noise her slippered feet made on the bare wooden stairs and the contrast with the total silence in the living room – despite the fact two adults sat there. She glanced outside at the Christmas-card scene and then caught her breath as she compared it with the unadorned room she now stood in. Both parents smiled wanly towards her. Her dad caught her looking at the wall clock which contained the day's date, and said,

"I know. It's been exactly..."

Suddenly, there was a loud knock at the door!

For what seemed like ages, everyone either sat or stood transfixed, staring at the source of this interruption – the front door. In fact, Mr and Mrs Deans were still sitting on their separate armchairs and Molly was still standing in the living room at the bottom of the stairs when another knock came. This time, Molly thought that the rata-tat-tat was quite rhythmic, almost cheery. It had been so long since anyone had knocked on the door that Molly was still moving towards it when the playful rata-tat-tat sounded again. She opened the door sheepishly, not really sure who she was expecting to see on the other side. At first all she could see was a mass of colours: green, blue, red, yellow. They all appeared to be wrapped around presents – Christmas presents – of varying sizes. Molly was spellbound, her concentration only broken when a man's head appeared above the boxes and said, "Hi, there! You must be Molly."

The Deans were already on their feet, moving towards the tall man who was now in their house, setting down presents in their small hallway. Before they could speak, the young man suddenly spun around, smiling.

"And you must be Kathleen and Tommy."

He removed his right woollen glove and shook Mr Deans' hand warmly, before doing the same with Mrs Deans, kissing her on her left cheek! For a moment all three adults stared at each other, before the man turned again to Molly and, bending down, gave her a big hug.

"I can't believe what a big girl you are!"

Mr Deans finally spoke for them all. "I'm sorry… but… who are you?"

"Oh, goodness me. I am so sorry. I think I've left my manners at home. I'm Stephen's son, Dillon."

"My cousin Stephen?"

"The very one. I'm Dillon Deans!"

At this news, Dillon was cautiously ushered into the family's living room. It had been such a long time since the Deans had 'entertained', that every welcoming gesture which had once been so instinctive was now like an afterthought: "…Take off your coat… have a cup of tea… would you like to freshen up?..." Although they had lived a few streets from each other and had been great friends when they were boys, Tommy had lost touch with his cousin Stephen when the latter had moved to the United States many years ago. He had heard he was married, but didn't know much else. He was sorry to hear from Dillon that both his parents were now dead. He looked at the young man's eyes as he spoke about that and felt so sad for him. He also realised that it was the first time in a year that he had considered – outside his immediate family – that someone else had a 'story'. When Dillon produced photographs not just from the USA but old ones that included Stephen, Tommy and Michael – Tommy's brother – as young boys in the very street where Molly lived today, she heard something else she hadn't heard in the house for a year: laughter.

Dillon explained that he was only in Glasgow for a short time. He was catching a flight to London first thing tomorrow – Christmas Day – to spend the Christmas holidays with an old friend from his university days.

Then, without warning, he suddenly blurted out, "Hey, where on earth is your tree?"

Mr Deans started to say something, but Dillon was on his feet heading to, then returning from, the hallway, tearing at a long, rectangular package.

"Hey, it doesn't matter. Panic over."

He explained that he had seen the tree at a garden centre in the afternoon and had been rather taken with it. He hadn't been thinking straight, he told them, because when he phoned to tell his friends in London, not surprisingly they already had one. So this was perfect. Molly, who had been glancing nervously at her mother and father at first, was now totally caught up in Dillon's enthusiasm and was already leading him towards the tree's traditional presentation place in the corner opposite the silent television.

***

On a couple of occasions, Mr Deans appeared as if he was about to object, but Dillon seemed to sense this and either talked over him or handed him a decoration from yet another box he had brought in from the hallway. Mrs Deans had been similarly tentative at first, but now she was silently helping Dillon to wrap the fairy lights around the tree. Molly thought that her new friend must be some sort of magician, because within a short space of time the transformation was complete and there – instead of a bare corner of the room – was the world's prettiest Christmas tree. At Dillon's insistence, Molly switched on the lights to applause from two of the adults. Her smile beamed every bit as brilliantly as the white lights themselves.

Mr Deans was frowning again and Dillon seemed to read his thoughts:

"Oh, Tommy, I see what you mean. Something's missing."

Molly and Kathleen turned to Tommy and they could see immediately that, whatever it was that he was thinking, that certainly wasn't it.

"Of course. Presents!"

Dillon was back off down the hallway, returning almost immediately with four gift-wrapped items. Down on his knees now, he started to place them at the bottom of the tree. As he carefully arranged them, he looked at each label in turn.

"One for Tommy. One for Kathleen. One for Molly. And, of course, one for Beth."

Turning around and seeing three faces frozen in misery staring back at him, Dillon, for the first time since his arrival, stopped smiling.

It had taken a while for the silence to break, but when it did it came out fast and at times confusingly. Because the tale was so sad, one of the Deans would suddenly stop as if about to completely break down and cry, but then another member would take it up and eventually it reached its sad conclusion. Now it was Dillon's turn to stare sadly into space.

Mrs Deans' quivering voice broke the silence. "I still go back to where the accident happened. There was so much snow about at the time and rain afterwards that we never found her locket. It was quite cheap really. In fact, it had a little chip at the bottom of the heart shape on the front and a picture of all four of us inside. I used to say to her, 'See that chip… that means that one day you'll break…'. It's just sentimental, Dillon… that's all."

Tommy squeezed his wife's hand and they shared a little sad smile. Molly couldn't remember the last time she'd seen her parents touch. All too often she'd discovered her dad staring into space in the back garden, but he always ushered her away when she tried to comfort him. Same with her mum. Once, she'd come home from school to find her sobbing really hard on the living room floor, but when her mum noticed she was there, she suddenly stood up, wiped away her tears and started to ask her politely about her day. Silence was a natural state now.

Dillon apologised to the group. He said that he'd been selfish; talking about his mum and dad had helped him and now he just felt terrible because he had upset the very people who had lifted his spirits so much. Suddenly, the Deans family was around him: cuddling, patting, consoling the young man.

"I am so sorry," said Mr Deans. "You've come to me to pass on Christmas cheer despite your own problems, and I've just been so wrapped up in myself."

At this, Mr Deans suddenly stopped and turned his attention away from Dillon.

"Oh, God! Kathleen and Molly… that's what I've been…"

"Sshhh," interrupted Kathleen, and suddenly all three of them were huddled together, crying. They were all speaking and crying at the same time; but, Molly thought, this is much better than the awkward silences to which they were all now too accustomed. After a while, Dillon rose and thanked them for their hospitality, but said that he must go to his hotel now as time was getting on. However, the Deans wouldn't hear of it.

"No, no," Tommy was insisting. "You will leave from here tomorrow and go directly to the airport. You should be with your family tonight", and as he looked around to the two tear-stained but smiling faces, he said, "...and so should we!"

Molly went to bed in preparation for Christmas Day! She had told Dillon that she would make a special effort to get up early to see him off on the next part of his journey. But, just in case, she gave him an extra special tight hug. The adults sat up into the small hours, talking and sometimes crying, but always talking. Tommy talked about how he would have to somehow make things up to his young daughter. He sat facing the floor as he recounted to Dillon about how he'd told her last

Christmas there was no Santa and certainly no god – how could there be? He was ashamed of himself now. Dillon managed to calm him, telling him that Molly was obviously a very special little girl and she was a lot more resilient than either Tommy or Kathleen thought. Tommy remembered her talking about a doll. What was it called? He couldn't even remember. Before he got too upset, Dillon assured him that Molly would just be delighted with a little bit of fun tomorrow. And she'd be ecstatic whenever they got her the doll, any doll.

Suddenly, there was the sound of a car engine running outside and Dillon crossed the room and looked out of the front window. "That's my taxi!"

Both Kathleen and Tommy were sad. Dillon hadn't mentioned he'd sent for one.

"I knew you'd insist on driving me to the airport, but I'd feel a lot better if I knew you were all here together."

"Do you have to go just now?" Mrs Deans asked.

Tommy started, "I feel that you've been so generous and…"

"I'm going to stop you right there, Tommy," said Dillon. "I have had the most wonderful time. I wish I could stay longer, but..."

"You've promised your friends. Kathleen and I understand."

As they were making their way to the door, Mrs Deans suddenly realised that Dillon had no luggage! Everything that he'd struggled through the door with a few hours before was now occupying a place in the Deans' residence. Dillon seemed to read her mind and explained that his luggage was already in London; all he had to do now was join it. There was just time for another round of hugs and then the happy, smiling, waving hurricane that was Dillon disappeared around the corner. As they closed the outside door, both Deans caught their breath at the feeling of emptiness, but Tommy was determined that the positive mood would not pass.

"Right, Mrs Deans, let's get to bed. We've a big day ahead of us tomorrow and we need our sleep!"

And sleep they did. Better than usual. Occasionally, one of them would wake and would begin to cry, but there would be no turning away from each other. No attempt to stifle their sorrow. Instead, one would gently rock and caress the other until the worst was over.

***

Kathleen Deans awoke with a start! A quick check of her tableside clock told her that Christmas morning was fast disappearing. And where was

Tommy? She leapt out of bed, but before she reached the bedroom door she stopped dead in her tracks. Something strange was going on. A nice strange. She could hear Christmas music blasting out, and yes, she was pretty sure that she could smell food! She made her way along the landing, passing Molly's open door and empty room. Just as she was beginning to go down the stairs, she froze for the second time that morning. She began to retrace her steps, wondering if she had imagined it. But no, as she stood back on the landing, she could see quite clearly that she hadn't. Beth's door was wide open. Not only that, she could make out clearly her double bed and the pop posters that adorned the wall. That was because a brilliant light was shooting through the curtains which hadn't been opened… in fact, those weren't even the curtains that had remained closed all this time!

After a few moments, she turned and again began a slow descent of the stairs.

When she reached the kitchen, both Tommy and Molly turned and rushed towards her. Tommy had been to the local corner shop to buy… well, anything to eat. And to buy his "two favourite girls" some chocolates. They would have to do for just now. Boxing Day he would take them out and make sure they got something a little more special. The smiles on the two girls' faces suggested he would be hard pushed to beat the pleasure they both felt at this particular moment. As they made their way through to the living room, the doorbell rang.

"Maybe Dillon's missed his plane," said Molly, as she ran to answer it.

Tommy smiled at Kathleen, but she noticed him brace himself for what was about to happen. Before she could figure out what was going on, Molly blurted excitedly, "It's Uncle Michael and Auntie Jean!"

Kathleen looked at Tommy for a brief second, before running off to warmly embrace first her brother-in-law and then his wife. Michael put down his many bags of presents and walked slowly towards his brother. He tried to speak, but Tommy grabbed him and pulled him close.

"I'm so sorry."

"No, Tommy, I'm the one…"

"No. No. Not at all. I know what kids are like. I know how much she loved you – both of you. What I've done is unforgiveable. Not speaking. There's no excuse…"

Michael was now sobbing uncontrollably. "There's not a day goes by when I don't wish it had been me instead."

Now everyone was in tears. Tommy spoke again. "Right. Enough. Today we'll laugh and probably cry some more, but we'll do it together – as a family. Now, you've brought overnight bags? Good. Then you two can sleep in Beth's room. Now don't look at me like that, it's what she would've wanted. Isn't that right, Kathleen?"

Mrs Deans smiled at her husband and said, "Definitely!"

"Good. Now, Michael, don't take your boots off yet. You, me and Molly are going across to help fix Fred Talbot's decorations. The Big Santa's loose again."

By the time he finished his sentence, Molly was running in from the kitchen with her boots already on and struggling with her coat.

***

Later in the evening, the group sat around the warm glow of the fire, relaxing with a drink. Molly was getting tired. She'd had a long, happy-sad but thoroughly lovely day. Just as she was about to go upstairs to put on her pyjamas, she stopped, as if remembering something. Mr Deans spotted this and asked what the problem was. At first she just shook her blonde curls and went to continue towards the stairs, but he gently coaxed her back. He explained that even when they were sad, they weren't ever going back to the days when silence ruled the house. Emboldened by this, Molly pointed out that there was a present that still hadn't been opened.

It was true. Michael and Jean had handed their gifts out and Molly had got her 'practical' clothes from her mum and dad, with the promise of something more exciting to come tomorrow! Tommy and Kathleen had – at Molly's insistence – opened their boxes from Dillon and had been delighted with their sets of matching woollen hats, scarves and gloves. Equally, Molly had loved her Bank Set, playing happily all day with the fake money and pretend customers. However, Molly was talking about the one present that hadn't been opened: Dillon's gift for Beth.

Mrs Deans said, "Oh, Molly, I don't know…"

"Oh, come on," her husband interrupted. "I think Beth would want us to open it."

As soon as her mum nodded in her direction, Molly reached under the tree and pulled the gift-wrapped box towards herself. By this time, Michael had moved over to sit on the floor beside Tommy to get a better view of Molly opening the present.

"You know, Tommy, I've been thinking…"

"Dad!" Molly shouted. "That's funny…"

"What is, sweetheart?"

"The label doesn't say 'Beth'; it's addressed to me."

She handed the Christmas label to her dad and continued with the unwrapping.

"Anyway," continued Michael, "I wasn't aware that…"

"Mum, there's a little envelope with your name on it. It's stuck to the inside of the box."

Molly handed the little envelope to her mum and continued with her own unwrapping.

"…. Stephen had any children. Not that I'd…"

"Wow!" shouted Molly. "That's amazing! Look, everyone, it's Perfect Polly, the doll I wanted for Christmas."

Tommy, Michael and Jean stared at the beaming child and the lovely-looking doll. No one noticed that Kathleen had moved across to the hallway and was opening the front door. As she moved outside, the local choir was just beginning *Silent Night*. She glanced at the bright surroundings. For a fleeting second her eyes fell on a familiar face. She smiled and moved her hand towards the locket around her neck. Then the face was gone. She turned back towards the inside of the house and shouted, “Right, you lazy lot. Get out here. They’re singing our Beth’s favourite carol.” Within seconds, everyone else was around her, including Tommy, who had brought out her coat and new woollen set. She hugged Molly tightly. Then all the Deans sang along lustily with the choir; not always in tune, but together!

The Return

Elspeth Gordon was standing at the bus stop with her two friends. They all loved this ten minutes – particularly on a Friday. They were now in their sixth year at high school and shared few classes, so the walk to – and the wait for – the bus gave them time to talk and share any gossip. That is, gossip that couldn't wait to be *tweeted*, *Face-Timed* or *posted on Facebook* in an hour or so. Friday was different, though. On Friday they made plans to meet up later – around about eight – always at one of their houses.

As the bus drew up, the three friends hugged one another so earnestly that anyone watching would think they were destined to spend a great deal of time apart. As the other two schoolgirls hopped on to the bus, Elspeth confirmed one last time that she would see them both later.

Samantha Jones waved one last time to Elspeth, showed her bus pass to the driver and then followed her friend up to the upper-deck. Her bright brown eyes darted about, trying to locate a double seat. With none available, she sat on the outside of a ‘half-occupied’ seat about six from the back. Her friend was across the aisle, three seats back. As it was difficult to hear what her friend was saying, she gave up trying to have a conversation, smiled and settled herself, facing towards the front of the bus. Samantha was staring beyond her seating ‘partner’, out of the window, absent-mindedly watching people going about their everyday lives. The soft, gentle rays of the afternoon sun caressed her face and she closed her eyes. Her moment of blissful peace was short-lived, however.

Emily Daly was at the back window of the bus, hammering her fists off it and alarming everyone, especially the two passengers who had no choice but to lean in opposite directions as she approached so aggressively. She shouted. She screamed. Samantha was behind her now. Scared. Terrified for her friend.

Emily swung around, her long black hair flowing wildly. Samantha tried to hold her, but Emily’s intense blue eyes showed how futile that was. She easily broke away from her friend, who had followed her down the stairs. Emily seemed to be heading towards the driver, but then decided against it when she realised he had begun to pull over to the next bus stop. Samantha followed as her friend took off, heading back in the direction from which they had just come. Eventually, drained, she stopped and pleaded with Emily to do likewise. After a few more strides, her friend did stop and looked back towards her.

"It's him," she shouted hoarsely. "It's him."

***

Margaret Daly was pacing back and forth between the front window of her lounge and her kitchenette. Her cold coffee sat on the breakfast bar, as she once again glared accusingly at the mounted wall clock. Each movement of the second hand reverberated throughout the house. It was 6.24pm. Emily was usually home around 4.20pm. If Samantha hadn't phoned, she'd have thought that Emily had something on after school – although that was unlikely on a Friday. She had contemplated driving towards where she knew her daughter had last been seen, but had abandoned that idea in case she missed her or in case Emily was to contact her at home. She had already begun pacing back towards the front window when she heard someone come in through the front door and enter the lounge.

Although it was only a few steps, Margaret quickened her pace and then let out an audible sigh as she pulled her shocked and distraught-looking daughter to her chest. She held her tight. She held her tight and told Emily that everything would be okay. After all, her daughter could talk to her about anything. She could – couldn't she? Emily was sobbing now. Gripping her mother tightly. Margaret reciprocated with more tight hugs and reassuring whispers. When she felt her daughter's grief, worry – whatever this was – subside ever so slightly, she eased her away. Although tearful herself, Margaret looked soothingly at her daughter. If Emily wanted to speak, she would. If she didn't – then fine. She should take as long as she needed. Emily wanted to. Very much. But when she tried to speak, she was so excited her mother found it hard to decipher her words. Yes, she'd seen someone – that much was clear. But who? And why was she so upset? Margaret sat her down on the sofa and rubbed her arms, waiting once again for her daughter's impassioned sobs to end. Emily took a deep breath.

"It was my dad," she sobbed. "My dad. Mum… he's alive."

Margaret held her tightly. She stroked Emily's long, black hair gently. She settled her daughter. She consoled her daughter. She was sympathetic; never patronising. She listened patiently to her daughter describing who she had seen. How she had been staring out of the right-hand side of the bus window. She hadn't been staring at anything in particular. But then, when the bus was stopped – due to the Friday traffic – she saw a man looking in the window of Lane's Bakery. She was looking at him, but she'd no idea why. Then, just as the bus began to move off, he turned around. Turned around and looked at the bus she was on. For a while it just didn't register with her. How could it? Her dead father back from the grave. Suddenly, though, she knew. She knew it was him. She scrambled to the back seat of the bus and thrashed against the window with her fists, but he was already heading away. Heading back up Muir Street in the opposite direction to the bus. She'd got off as quickly as possible and headed in *his* direction. But she couldn't find him. She'd looked in all of the shops. All of them – including the bars – but he wasn't there. He'd disappeared. Again. Then she started to ramble on some more about how he may have got into a car. Driven away. Who knows? Just gone. Again.

If Margaret Daly had learned anything about her seventeen years as a mum – particularly the last nine as a single parent – it was knowing when to speak up, and when to say nothing. Now was a time to do the latter. Now was a time to continue to console and cajole her daughter and try to bring her back to some state of calm and normality. For some time after Paul's death, Emily had woken up in the middle of the night screaming. It had taken her a long time to come to terms with her father's death, but surely that was natural. She'd never had an episode like this one before.

Throughout the evening, mother and daughter had talked and cried and then talked and cried some more. Margaret had fielded calls from Elspeth and Samantha, who both pointed out that Emily must be in a bad way as she'd never missed a 'Friday night' before. Eventually, around eleven, an exhausted Emily had gone to bed to fall into a deep, restful sleep. Margaret looked at her daughter from the doorway, wishing she could take away from her any pain or confusion. She whispered one last "God Bless" and slowly pulled the door shut.

Back downstairs, she sat at the breakfast bar trying to relax and to contemplate all that had happened on this strange day. In front of her sat a half-full glass of Merlot and her mobile phone. She stared at both, trying to decide which one to reach for first.

***

Ian Wilson threw his black suit jacket over the back of his leather couch. As he walked towards the kitchen area, he pulled at his blue silk tie and opened the top button of his white shirt. He opened a cupboard door at head height in his fitted kitchen and took out a Lismore tumbler, then turned his attention to the freezer compartment of his fridge. He took out two blocks of ice and dropped them unceremoniously into the glass. He wandered back through the open-plan flat to his lounge area. He paused at a small, round table, lifted the bottle on it, poured himself a generous measure of Lagavulin and looked out through the long window at the city lights. He loved the view afforded by the penthouse apartment – particularly at this time of night. Today had been especially busy. So much so that when he looked at his phone, he realised for the first time that he had nine messages on *Voicemail.* Not wishing to interrupt his calm mood, he laid his phone on the table, switched it on to speaker mode and continued with his view of the city – and the sipping of his whisky.

***

He flicked through November's *Golf Monthly* for the third time. He wasn't really paying attention. He didn't even like golf. He certainly hadn't played it in the last seven years. Why, oh why, were the magazines so outdated? Looking around the room didn't actually take his mind off things, either. Yes, the pastel green walls didn't bring on any angst or any sort of anxiety attack, but was that just because they were so bland? Holding on to the bottom of his chair, he began to gently rock back and forth. Then he stood up and walked over to the fish tank. He enjoyed looking at the different shapes and colours, but he couldn't identify a single one of the species. Not if his life had depended on it. Behind him, the door of the small waiting room opened.

"Mr Newman," smiled the receptionist, "Doctor Grant will see you now."

***

The first two messages had been from business associates and barely registered. Third and fourth had come from Lynn – his secretary – and were reminders about tasks he had still to complete before the weekend finished. *What would I do without her?* Fifth was from another business associate and seemed to go on and on. And on. While only half-listening, he refilled his glass and held it up towards the city, in a silent toast to Lynn. The sixth was from his daughter and brought a reassuring smile. No need to panic. No need to feel guilt. He had already spoken to her earlier in the day. She was just confirming Sunday's lunch *date*. As the seventh message played, he froze. Still as stone.

***

She felt better now. Things *did* always seem better in the morning. Hearing her daughter close the bathroom door, Margaret began to unpack the croissants and switch the oven on low. She really did feel better as she watched a bright-eyed, happy Emily bounce towards the breakfast bar.

"Is that my favourite vanilla coffee I smell?"

"It certainly is. Croissants and strawberry jam okay?"

Emily didn't answer, but stretched across to where her mum was standing and kissed her on the cheek. She then apologised to her mum.

"What for?"

Emily said that it was for all the distress that she had caused the previous night. She realised now just how upsetting for her mum it must have been. Margaret, for her part, pointed out that her only concern was for Emily. The two chatted some more. Just general chit-chat. The mother was prepared to talk about everything – anything – until the daughter was ready. Eventually, Emily apologised again. Again Margaret reassured her.

"I was so sure it was him. So sure. I know it seems crazy."

Her mum squeezed her hand. Emily couldn't offer any rational explanation. It *was* crazy. Then she was giggling, before laughing uproariously at how idiotic she must have seemed to those people on the bus – and the shopkeepers! Now they were both laughing. No sooner had they agreed to a little *retail therapy*, when the doorbell rang. Margaret answered and led a concerned-looking Elspeth and Samantha into the spacious lounge. Their worry quickly dissipated when they saw how lively and happy Emily looked. Then the two girls breathlessly explained that they had come to cheer up their best pal by taking her into town. Emily hugged the two and thanked them, but said that she already had plans – with her mum. Margaret overheard and insisted that she go with her friends – they would go out another day. Emily began to protest, but her smiling mum was firm.

"No! You go with the girls, Emily. I'll be fine. Honestly. I've got something else to do."

***

"It's been a long time."

"Seven months?"

"Almost ten. Why the sudden need to see me? Are you okay?"

"I'm fine. I think I'm fine…"

"Just think?"

"No… I *am* fine. I feel fit… healthy…"

"But?"

"I don't know. Yesterday…"

"What about it?"

"I really don't know… I had to go to Glasgow yesterday. A client – a big client – had got a delivery in the morning and was short. Just a gallon tin, that was all. I know, the distance! But they needed it. So the boss asked me did I fancy a wee trip. Take his car, deliver the paint asap and then take my time coming back. I dropped it off in the city centre. No problems. Everybody happy."

"No hassle from the company?"

"No. I delivered it straight to the site and the guy on the job was delighted just to have it. On the way back I avoided the motorway. No rush, and it was such a nice day. About three-quarters of an hour outside the city I started to hit some heavy traffic – slowed right down. I glanced to my right and spotted this shop – a bakery. Don't ask me what it was about it, because I can't explain. I drove on a bit, parked and went back on foot. Looked in the window. Nothing. There were two ladies inside, as far as I could see."

"Did you go inside?"

"No. Just window-shopped. I started to head back in the direction I had driven. But nothing. It was only at the shop I felt something. I just don't know what. I noticed it was about four, so I headed back with the boss's car."

"And then?"

"And then – I phoned you."

***

Wilson looked around the *old* streets. Nothing much had changed. Not really. He stood before the Oxfam store, but looked to the flat above.

Incredible, really. Five of us had lived in there. Five. And not the flat it was now. He had been involved in smashing through walls, creating two more bedrooms and a fitted kitchen – and a bathroom. *Luxury*, he laughed to himself: *luxury*! Not like when his mum had to take all sorts of jobs to pay over the odds in rent for the one-bedroom flat it had once been. She had been prepared to do anything to escape his abusive, alcoholic father. It had been his job to look after his three sisters. When his mum wasn't there, he fed them, made sure they were clean and tidy – and that their homework, as well as his, was done. Never regretted it. Poor mum. She'd done everything she could for them. Everything. Then that bloody disease had taken her before she could enjoy the fruits of her many labours. He glanced once more at the front of the building before he moved on. *What would I do to avoid going back there? Anything*. And he knew he meant it.

***

He had the train ticket in his hand – bought and paid for – yet still he stood at the end of the platform. This was only the second train that *ran* to Glasgow on a Saturday. He hadn't taken the previous one – though he had had time to spare after he had purchased the ticket. What was he thinking? Didn't everyone have episodes that they put down to déjà vu? For him, though, it was different. The last seven years had been difficult. But he could remember them – generally. The previous two years before that? Well, they were… hazy at best. The sudden movement of the electronic clock above the entrance to the platform propelled him from his thoughts: 1400. Five minutes to departure time. What to do…?

***

He didn't see her at first when he entered the coffee house. Finally spotting her at one of the tables towards the back wall, he noticed how tense she looked. He would have to calm her. Reassure her. Just as he had always done. He caught the waitress's eye, ordered a latte and another mineral water. They talked about everything and nothing for several minutes. Then she looked away. He put his hand on hers.

"Why so worried? Emily herself realises it's just a daft mistake."

"Why? Because when you finally called me back about half-past one this morning, you didn't sound convinced. For the first time in nine years, you weren't convincing."

"I was upset… upset for you… and for Emily."

"No."

"Yes. That was all. A bit guilty maybe."

"It's a bit late for that. You did well out of it!"

"We all did."

She looked apologetic now. She'd overstepped the mark.

"I'm sorry."

"It's okay."

"No, it's not. Big brother to the rescue as ever, eh?"

He smiled, sat back and drank his coffee.

"Always."

***

Tommy Macgregor took one last gulp from his glass of Bollinger Sp Reserve and wiped his mouth with his napkin.

"Good drop that. Italian is it?"

"Australian," one of the men opposite replied acerbically.

"Well, you have my terms if you…"

"Yeah, we have them. Goodnight."

Macgregor eyed his two dinner companions for a few seconds, then stood up. The third man stood, too.

"I'll see you out."

The two men waited just inside the front door as the driver – who had been parked on the other side of the street from the restaurant – swung the

MP's car around, bringing it to a halt directly outside Albert's. Wilson reassured him.

"I'll speak to him. He'll be fine."

"That's up to you. This extension of the Waterfront Project is going to be the biggest thing ever to hit Glasgow. All the big hitters are lined up. We go back a long way, that's why I wanted to deal you in."

"We are in, Tommy. Believe me – we're in. I'll be in touch by the end of the week."

"Good. Make sure you are."

Wilson waved to Macgregor from the kerbside, then turned to look at the restaurant. He'd already tried to persuade his partner that this was how business was done. He shook his head. He had no hope of getting him to change his mind.

***

He looked at the countryside passing by in a blur outside. He turned to his female travelling companion and smiled.

"How did you know I'd need a shove?"

"I could tell you were unsure. And it's not a shove, it's a… gentle nudge."

***

He held her hand on the table and smiled.

"Do you want a lift home?"

"No, ta. I'm going to pick up a few things for our tea, then get the train home."

"I think I'll join you. I could do with the fresh air."

***

Having her beside him had really helped him relax. What a lady. She'd been due to have a well-earned rest for a change, but here she was on the train to Scotland with him. Just like that. He looked at her sleeping. So peaceful. So lovely. And everything she did for him – unconditional. She didn't even know who he was. That was something that they had in common. What did he know? Apparently, he'd wandered into a homeless shelter in London eight years ago. Later on, she had arranged for him to see Dr Grant. After several sessions with him, he had some sketchy recollections of dossing down in the street and in another shelter the previous year, but that had been all. Before that: nothing. Not until he'd come across that little bakery shop, at least. Jill had wanted him – no, that wasn't true – she had asked him if he wanted to put his picture onto a social networking site like Twitter or Facebook. He wasn't really sure why he declined. He was certainly curious, but he always felt some sort of…

of what? He wasn't sure that it was fear, but there was certainly something that held him back from taking that step: back into his past.

***

Paul Daly made his way downstairs after making sure his daughter Emily was 'tucked in' and after giving her a *goodnight* kiss. When he entered the small living room, the atmosphere was a great deal frostier than in his only child's bedroom. His brother-in-law had left while he had been upstairs. He'd always thought that Margaret and he had made a great team. So she had surprised him earlier when she had sided opposite him. He was taken aback, too – though he fought hard not to show it – when she disclosed details of the Waterfront Project. Details that *he* had not shared with her. He had thought it a *no-brainer*: he didn't mind occasionally wining and dining various planning committee members. He saw that as part of the job. However, this level of payment to a Member of Parliament to *get in the game* was a whole different level of corruption. It was just plain wrong – and he thought she'd feel the same. He thought they'd always be reading from the same page. He was disappointed. Maybe the old saying about blood and water was true after all.

***

She stopped just before they reached the steps which led to Platform 2. Even after their pleasant walk in the early summer sunshine, she was still perplexed.

"When I phoned."

"What about it? I told you. Bad memories. I felt guilty. I *feel* guilty. I *still* feel guilty."

She nodded, climbed four steps, then stopped again. She turned to her brother and looked him directly in the eyes.

"It was more than that."

***

Now they were standing on Platform 2. It was funny. Sitting beside him, she had felt the tension in him rise, the further the train travelled north. The train would be making only three stops on the way to Glasgow – all towards the end of the journey. So anxious did he seem, she'd half expected him to leap up at the first opportunity – but he hadn't. However, as the train approached this station, he'd given her a little smile and raised his eyebrows, as if to ask her permission to disembark. She had smiled understandingly and now here they were.

***

Wilson tried to avoid the disbelieving and searching eyes of his sister. There *had* been some kind of mistake. He didn't know what had happened. The so-called crash, the blazing car, it just wasn't how it was supposed to happen. He'd always assumed it had been Paul in the car, but Macgregor had pulled a few strings to get what was left of the body back quickly. He guessed some checks had either been rushed or quietly left alone. Either way, they had a body. Then weeks went by and there had been no word from Samuels. Not a peep! A *contracts* man who had forgotten to collect the other half of his *reward*? His sister was backing away from him now. As she turned to walk through the gap between wall and fence that led on to the platform, Wilson caught her by the arm. Didn't she see that he'd had the same thoughts? For weeks, then months, then years he'd been waiting for the call or the knock at the door – but it never came. Now he was certain: Paul was dead! Yes, it had been a shock yesterday, Emily seeing someone that looked like him – nine years ago – looking into the shop you worked in when you had first met. But that's all. A shock. "I mean, why wouldn't he have come back before? He'd have wanted revenge, surely? He'd have wanted to see Emily – and you. He never knew about you."

***

They held each other tight.

"Are you sure?"

"Definitely! You okay?"

"Of course. Hey, it's not every day that a girl gets a 'new' man."

"True. But I'm not sure about the *Paul*, though."

"Well tough. I got to pick. And it's the name of my mum's favourite actor!"

"I am flattered."

They linked arms and headed towards the *bridge* that led across the tracks to Platform 1. Jill saw a couple, looking quite agitated, just outside the entrance. She nodded towards them, saying,

"See, it's not just us that's got problems."

***

Margaret had tears in her eyes now, but she was listening to him. It made sense. At least the bit about *him* being dead. They turned and walked onto the platform just as a train on the opposite side pulled in.

***

"Are you sure?" asked Jill again.

"Definitely. Times two."

***

Ian cupped his sister's chin in his hand. He looked at her soothingly. The way he had always done throughout their lives. *That* way that told Margaret that everything would be just fine.

***

On board the train, opposite, a couple held hands and smiled warmly at each other.

"No regrets?"

"None. If my old life is somewhere back there, then it couldn't have been that great. No one's come looking for me. It couldn't have been better than it is now. I owe you so much: the job…"

"Ssshhh. I'm the lucky one."

Then Jill lent in to him and kissed him on the lips. As they broke off, they both smiled. Jill glanced out of the window and spotted the couple she had seen earlier, looking much more content now.

"What do you think their story is?" she said, nodding towards the platform opposite.

Paul stared hard at them.

"Hmmm. Husband and wife… a wee bit of distance between them, though. An argument, I think!"

"Ha, ha. I told *you* that bit. More brother and sister. They're close, but… no, not married."

As the train doors closed, Paul leaned forward again.

"Yeah. You're right. Brother and sister. I can see a resemblance."

As the train slowly moved off, Paul kissed Jill again.

"I know one thing for sure. They don't have what we have."

Got the One and Only...

The four bright colours happily trudged through the snow towards their destination. Eventually, with the giant illuminated snowman in sight, the smaller green and yellow hues broke away from the larger red and blue, their little legs disappearing, then, almost as quickly, re-emerging from the perky white cotton-coloured pavements. No sooner had the children let out their excitable squawks of delight, than the front door sprung open in welcome. Seven people spilled out onto the bleached turf, mingling so quickly with the four new arrivals that within seconds they were one happy, shiny blur. Eventually, they moved en-masse towards the entrance of the house. It appeared that the Christmas Day celebrations would continue inside now. Never at any stage did anyone notice, or seem even remotely aware of, the figure at the window of the first-floor flat opposite who had been watching the scene, and other scenes just like it, throughout the day.

The sharp *Ping* pulled him from his trance and he turned back from the window and sighed at the contrast the dull room made with the happy, vibrant scenes outside. Yet he had at least made an effort. Hadn't he?

The tree was up, at least. Small, yes; but quite cute, surely? Artificial, true; but the silver – silver-ish – fir with the one remaining branch brightened up the room no end. Something wasn't right, though. He wondered if he should have replaced the single gold bauble. Maybe, but he'd had it since… well, since… a while. Lights! Yes, suddenly all was clear now. The problem was staring him in the face. He had decorated the tree with lights, but with only a single, microscopic blue bulb flashing – like some miniature police car pursuing a tiny suspect or on the way to buy doughnuts. The effect was not spectacular. Behind it he noticed the brown tape held against the dark mustard wall by a single drawing pin at either end: now that *is* a match, he thought. He wasn't sure if the card was dead centre, though. He walked over to it, flipped up the front with his index finger and nodded approvingly: *Happy Christmas to all our customers. From Mr Ming.*

He had gotten a very smart Chinese calendar, too – for the British New Year, of course. Now that was good customer service. He gave them his trade; they showed their appreciation on special occasions. Staring at the card and the name *Ming*, he suddenly frowned; he'd forgotten the reason he'd turned his attention back to the inside of the house. The *Ping*. The microwave *Ping* that signalled his Christmas Dinner – turkey and peas and carrots – was ready. He sat down in his favourite chair, which was positioned right in front of his twenty-inch television screen. Good timing. *Dave* had been tuned in and *Only Fools and Horses* – Christmas special 1983, a classic – had just begun: No Income Tax. No V.A.T. His first bite into his turkey, though, brought his nostalgic reverie to a sudden halt. It wasn't very warm. While he was considering whether to put the whole meal back into the microwave or not, he heard more revelry from outside. He walked over to the window and saw the Wildes making their way next door to the Shaws'. Nice. It's good when neighbours are friends. He watched ruefully until the last Wilde child, no doubt weighed down with some frankincense, disappeared into the warm bosom of the Shaws' family home. Suddenly, he was on full alert. The surprise had shaken him, frozen him; but now he was moving: clumsily, quickly, because the shrill ring of the phone was demanding his immediate attention.

Lack of care, inelegant movement and a dearth of space combined to send him tumbling over the one easy chair in the room. Desperation pushed him towards his goal. Like a soldier on manoeuvres, he crawled quickly along the floor, before reaching out and pulling on the cable of the phone, which sat on the waist-high table. He caught the handset in both hands, but the base clattered onto his face. Undeterred, he began blurting into the handset.

"Hello. Hello. Happy Christmas. Happy Christmas. Oh, thank you. You, too… you're… Ah… I see. No, it's Noel here. Oh, don't worry, you haven't… merry Christmas to you, too."

No sooner had he sadly replaced the phone back on the table when he heard more merriment – from outside. Great. No, seriously, it *was* great. Great that the Wordsworths had more guests arriving. After all, it would be awfully quiet if no one had visited them. How would the seven of them have coped on their own? Why, it didn't bear thinking about.

Remorsefully, he turned away from the window and shook his head. It didn't help: his being bitter. He looked at the cold, depressed-looking Christmas meal and then towards *Rodders*. He had to escape. Without even bothering to switch off the television or the Christmas lights – Christmas *light* – he picked up his brown bomber jacket from the back of the chair and headed towards his front door.

Walking along the snow-covered street, he felt the icy chill cuff his face and head. It was slightly painful, but it seemed to energise him, too. A great benefit of everyone else having somewhere to go was that the streets were deserted. Even when he reached Main Street, all he could make out was a sea of untouched snow stretching beyond him.

He was growing into this 'adventure' now. He was actually enjoying himself. That was until he passed Milwards. Even then he continued for about a dozen steps before coming to a complete halt. He stared ahead as if trying to comprehend what he had just seen. Maybe he should just walk on. Eyes fixed straight ahead. But he couldn't. That wouldn't be right. He took a deep breath and turned back towards the alley which ran alongside the dress shop. He peered through the darkness and saw 'it' again. There was no mistake. Unfortunately.

He edged ever closer. The black tarpaulin having been blown aside, no longer did it cover: the body. Poor soul. What a way to go. What a time of year to go. He was about to head home to call the police; he really had to invest in one of those mobile phones. After all, wouldn't one be ideal for this sort of thing? He stopped, though. What if this poor soul was still alive? He couldn't simply walk away. Nervously, he stood over the sheet. *How am I going to do this? Like a plaster.* Taking an extra deep breath, he reached down and pulled the cover away from the body. He leapt backwards, the open eyes of the 'victim' making him want to turn and run. He stopped himself – just. He turned back once more. Poor girl. Poor… mannequin?

He was laughing now. How could he have been so stupid? Quite easily, really. Even now it looked so lifelike, in her-its-trendy floral dress and red shoes. The long, curly brown hair was another excellent addition. He stood up and headed towards Main Street again, still laughing noiselessly to himself. *She* had seemed so real. Especially in this light. Even when he was just a few steps away. It would be impossible to make out that it was a mannequin from the other side of the road. *The other side of the road.* He stopped, turned around and headed back towards the fallen figure in the snow-covered alleyway.

The festivities were in full swing when he returned to the Close. Through each brightly lit window he could see a kaleidoscope of colours and hear the muffled sounds of *Slade*, *Wizzard* and *Bing Crosby*. He was aware that those in the houses couldn't see him – or his companion. That wasn't good. He didn't want them to have a clear view, but it was imperative – if his plan was to be successful – that they could make him out through the darkness. But what to do?

Quickly, he made his way across the road and stood just outside the Shaws' fence. After quickly checking that the surrounding area was still deserted, he made a large snowball and threw it towards the living room window. Bullseye! He started to turn away, but quickly realised there had been no reaction from inside. No-one was coming forward to investigate. No-one. Now he leaned his new 'friend' carefully against the street lamp and gathered a huge ball of snow. Straining, he lifted the large white orb above his head and hurled it with all his might. Too short. The gigantic snowball made contact with the wall beneath the window, before sliding dismally to the ground. Another quick check told him he was still the only person outside in the street. He then climbed clumsily over the Shaws' tall wrought-iron fence – before spotting the easily accessible gate – and made his way stealthily towards the former projectile. From what he could make out, the party revellers were standing away from the area inside the window and no-one had noticed the man outside in the biting cold wearing an *I don't like Christmas...* T-shirt marauding around the front garden. He inched back towards the fence and peered through the gaps. Still no-one. He nodded through the fence to his date – still slumped against the lamp post – and turned back, ready to complete his task.

He rolled the snow mound once more, returning it back to its former round shape. He remembered the gate and quickly glanced around, wanting to ensure that he could reach it quickly and get outside the garden before those inside had made it to the window. Then, hopefully, from that same window, they could observe him out on the other side of the street, heading home with his special lady.

He crouched down and began to lift the giant snowball. It took a great deal of effort to lift the huge orb above his head. Like a weightlifter – albeit in the Winter Olympics – he felt his legs begin to buckle, but he held on. Slowly, he rose triumphantly to his full height. Totally composed. Then, just as he was about to 'fire', he stopped. Dead. Somebody, *something*, was there in the garden with him. About thirty paces to his left, he became aware of it: watching him. Something small. Maybe the family's toddler… or maybe… maybe the family's Devil Dog. The family's Hell Hound.

The low-level *grrr* acted like a hard slap across his cold cheeks. He dropped the giant snowball and rushed for the gate. He didn't need to see the Bullmastiff charge as he could hear it gallop, scattering the snow, as it powered in his direction. He reached the gate, but sensed his attacker's arrival was imminent, so he leapt high upon the gate, his trailing left foot escaping the slobbering jaws of his nemesis by inches. Emboldened by this rush of adrenaline, another leap saw him swing around the top of the gate: the white-coloured words on the back of his T-shirt –*I love it* – were no more than a blur across the night sky. Even the chasing dog must have felt this first part of the manoeuvre had been performed admirably; impressively, even.

However, every performer should understand that pride often precedes a fall. And so it was. As our gallant performer was mentally congratulating himself on his nimble movement on – and over – these particular parallel bars, his lack of concentration was transmitted to his right hand, which had been holding onto the bar at the top of the gate, and his grip and balance were lost all at once and he hurtled backwards, towards the ground.

He landed with a dull thump on the heavy snow. Half-startled, he sat up and realised that the Shaws' front door was opening and someone was shouting to the dog, concerned that it was okay. The acrobatic display seemed to have stunned the once-belligerent Bullmastiff, and it sat, panting face against the gate, looking at the unlikely gymnast. The pair gazed deep into each other's eyes. He allowed himself a brief, indulgent grin. The dog's eyes fixed on him with an intensity which seemed to say: *Next Time*. As he began to get to his feet, though, he realised that Rolfe – like his Austrian namesake with the von Trapps – was not prepared to let bygones be bygones and let him disappear into the night with an understated auf wiedersehen. Instead, he turned towards his own house and let out a huge howl. He then turned back to the man and seemed to flash a self-satisfied, smug grin, before unleashing more frantic yelps.

The 'intruder' didn't witness the fact that a throng was now pushing out of the Shaws' front door in an attempt to see what was upsetting Rolfe. He had been too busy grabbing his 'lady' and pulling her across to the other side of the road. He managed to compose himself just as the spectators took their places, faces pressed against the railings inside the Shaws' garden. He moved away from any light, keeping his 'friend' on his left side. Mr Shaw grinned:

"It's okay, folks. Looks like Noel gave poor Rolfe a bit of a fright."

The crowd laughed and began to head back inside. However, Mrs Wilde lingered outside and, still staring outwards onto the street as Noel turned into the pathway which led to his flats, shouted over to Mr Shaw:

"Is that a woman with Noel?"

Just before he closed the outside door leading to the stairway to his first-floor flat, Noel was pretty sure that he heard his name float across the white desert street: twice. He smiled. Rabid dog aside, his plan had gone well.

Once inside, being a gentleman, he removed his jacket from the 'lady's' shoulders and hung it on the door handle. When he looked out across the snowy street, he noticed that a small group was still in the Shaws' garden. Not only that, they were looking in the direction of his flat. He grinned. Time for phase two. At that, he moved his mannequin over to… mannequin… mannequin. That wasn't right. If this manne… lady was helping him out by showing his neighbours that he was far from the boring fuddy-duddy that they seemed to believe he was, then the least he could do was show her some respect. And, what better place to start than to give her a name. Hmm. What, though? Dolly? Barbie? Too obvious. Maybe call her Angela, after my mother? No. That's just weird. My Little Pony? Even weirder. Besides, nowadays modern women have modern names. Don't they? He felt 'she' needed a modern name. Unusual, yeah, with maybe a hint of this time of year. Mary? Too obvious. Tinsel? Too ridiculous. Jingles? Too… too right. Jingles… Jingles. It's… it's modern. Yip, that was it. Modern with a festive twist. Brilliant. He positioned his modern, model girlfriend at the window and sighed.

"Jingles, can I get you a drink?"

Across the street, there was no sign of the small gathering dissipating. They were still staring up towards the window on the first floor, not quite sure what to make of it all. Yes, that had been Noel Winter making his way to his home not ten minutes ago. And yes, he was definitely arm-in-arm with a woman. A very stylish, glamorous woman at that.

Boring Noel? The guy who didn't have any friends? The guy who never had any visitors? That Noel! Incredible.

"She looked a bit of all right."

Mrs King punched her husband hard on the arm, causing him to flinch, then rub the affected area. Mr Wilde turned to Mr Shaw.

"You don't suppose we've got this guy wrong, do you, Ernest?" Mr Shaw shook his head, but without much conviction. "What about you, Oscar?"

Mr Hemingway looked deep in thought. "Maybe."

Across the street, Noel and Jingles were toasting each other – again. She had barely touched her ginger beer, but he was already on his second cut-price cola. In between sips and the odd naughty-but-nice-joke, Noel spotted that one of the group had broken away and was heading – oh my word – towards the entrance of his flat.

Ernest Shaw, always a man of action, had decided to attack the problem head-on. Now he was standing at Noel's front door, pushing with all his might on the impotent doorbell. Inside, Noel paced up and down, thinking, praying for some sort of solution to his predicament, before the silence turned to the rat-a-tat-tat of the letterbox and he made his way – slowly – to the door.

"Ernest! What a surprise. Happy Christmas."

Mr Shaw didn't reply immediately. He seemed to be looking past Noel, trying to catch a glimpse of… something or somebody. Suddenly, he seemed to remember where he was.

"Oh, yeah, right. Happy Christmas, Noel."

There then followed another period of silence, which was finally broken by Noel.

"Was there anything…?"

"No… eh… well, yes, actually. Senga, Mrs Shaw, was wondering if you would like to join us for some festive drinks and nibbles. You and eh…"

"Jingles."

"Jingles?"

"My girlfriend Jingles. You saw us come in."

"Yes… yes, of course. Jingles. Yes, you and Jingles should join us."

"That would be lovely. Jingles isn't feeling herself – bit of a cold – but we'll try to make it. Thank you." At that, Noel closed the door and walked back into his living room. Joining Jingles at the window, he watched Mr Shaw head back across the road to his house.

"Darling, would you mind? I'm going to pop over to the Shaws' for an hour." Noel took her silence as an assent and, after clinking his glass against hers, downed his cola in one gulp. He sighed happily – what a time to be alive!

On his arrival at the Shaws', he had had to work hard at ignoring the obvious disappointment of the gathering: that he had come alone. Being the last pick of the Charade Captains – even after the children – hadn't helped his feeling of seclusion. Nevertheless, he had thrown himself into the game wholeheartedly and the assembled throng began to warm to him. In fact, Ina Hemingway commented that she for one would never forget his mime for *Captain Fantastic and the Brown Dirt Cowboy*.

Eventually, Noel found himself relaxing and no longer felt conspicuous. He was no longer the awkward centre of attention; but, as the evening wore on, he was accepted as part of the company. A quick glance at the clock told Noel that he had passed his intended visit time by around an hour. He mused that it was true: time did indeed go quickly when you were enjoying yourself. For someone who had rarely been in the group's company before, it was only natural that conversation turned to the reason for his invite. Particularly when Mrs Shaw and Mrs Wilde cornered him by the wrap table.

"And Noel, how is… eh…?"

"Jingles? Oh, she's fine, bit of a cold."

"Oh, I had that all last week. Makes you feel all sore. I felt really stiff, I could hardly move."

"Oh, yeah, she's the same."

"It's a crying shame. What is it she does?"

"Does?"

"Yes. What does she work at?"

"Oh, she's in retail."

The questions about Jingles were starting to come thick and fast now and he was worried about saying something that would give away the real identity of his friend.

"She is really pretty, isn't she?"

Noel realised that with each question he was becoming a little more entrenched in his subterfuge. So he simply smiled back at Mrs Shaw. Surely that couldn't be deemed as lying? However, Mrs Wilde thought that she had picked up on a little evasiveness on his part and pressed on.

"Oh, she's gorgeous. Isn't she, Noel?"

Noel looked around for help, but he was trapped in an oral cul-de-sac. All he could do was look at his two pursuers and offer, "Yes, thank you. She's a doll."

After some further interrogation, he managed to sidle away and start to head for home. He managed to negotiate the front door and get outside without any fuss. He looked up and waved towards the figure in the window across the street. She didn't respond, remaining stoical. *She's a natural*, he thought. As he made his way up the freshly snow-covered path, he reflected on an excellent evening. Best Christmas – no, best night – he'd had in years. However, his jovial mood was brought to a crashing halt.

It wasn't because of something he had witnessed. No, the surrounding area looked – for the first time in a long time – quite beautiful. It wasn't about something that had been on his mind throughout the night. No – for the first time in… well, years, he'd had a lovely evening. No. It was a noise that had brought him out of his daydream. A noise that he'd heard just a few hours ago but had forgotten all about: until now. He turned towards it and found the smug, satisfied face of his canine nemesis: *Grrr*.

With two quick bounds, Rolfe was upon him, knocking him to the ground. Noel tried to push him off, but he found that the murderous mutt was not easy to shift. Noel thought that he had died because he could hear the voice of an angel. "Rolfe. Rolfe. Come here. Get off the nice man." The homicidal hound moved off – reluctantly – towards the voice.

Noel rolled onto his side, then pulled himself up onto both feet and found himself staring at Mrs Shaw's widowed sister: Grace Hathaway. "He's lovely, isn't he? Full of fun, but lovely."

Noel looked down at the Bullmastiff, who met his gaze. "Yeah. Full of fun." Through the darkness he watched as Grace led the dog around to the rear of the house. He turned towards the gate once again, but this time it was the pleasant voice of Grace that stopped him in his tracks

"You're not going, are you?"

He nodded towards his living room window. "Yeah. I'll need to get back. I didn't see you in the house."

Grace smiled. "No, I was in the kitchen when you arrived and then you were too busy with your pals." Noel smiled back at her. "I've actually been home a couple of months now. I stayed on a couple of years after Will… it just wasn't the same."

"Yeah, he was a good bloke."

Suddenly, the two were engulfed by the rest of the crowd, led by Mr Shaw.

"C'mon, you two. Time for the fireworks."

Noel tried to leave, but everyone insisted that he stay until they were finished, and when he continued to try to leave, it was pointed out to him that his 'date' had a fantastic view of the proceedings. So why rush back?

The Shaws and the Wildes and the Hemingways all let off various multi-coloured, multi-noised rockets, before finally Mr Shaw disappeared inside his house, only to re-emerge a few seconds later with a large, rectangular box. "Look at that: *Made in China*. This is the *Boom-Boom Giant*. The biggest rocket this side of NASA." Stopping only to laugh at his own joke, he set it up by digging his heel into the grass, then wedging the missile into the hole. "Now, let's all get right behind this, because this is gonna be big. Huge. Awesome." He then stepped forward and lit the fuse with his cigarette lighter. After he had stepped back, it appeared as if his efforts were all to be in vain. For a few seconds there was complete silence as everyone contemplated the possibility that *Boom-Boom* might just be a colossal *Dud-Dud*. However, just as Mr Shaw moved back towards it, a spark miraculously seemed to ignite and make its way up the rocket.

The crowd murmured their appreciation and anticipation. Then, just before it seemed about to take off, the rocket tilted forward and the horrified throng gasped as the missile exploded into life, hurtling with unerring accuracy towards Noel's front window – and Jingles.

In the ensuing panic, various people reached for their mobile phones as soon as *Boom-Boom* struck, all intent on one thing: to call the emergency services. What they couldn't understand was Noel's reticence about the whole thing. Hadn't he realised that *Boom-Boom* had blasted through his window and engulfed poor Jingles in flames?

The reason for his rather laid-back, matter-of-fact manner was revealed when two firefighters brought out a badly charred Jingles on a stretcher. The initially horrified crowd dissolved into fits of laughter when they realised the real condition of the victim. Noel turned to try and explain, but the crowd were already heading back to the Shaws', giggling and chortling as they went. A firefighter, the epitome of professionalism and tact, explained that there was only superficial damage to his living room. It was perfectly habitable. He then wished the beleaguered house owner a *Good Evening* and a *Merry Christmas*.

Noel was just about to head back inside, when he felt a tap on his shoulder. He turned and found Grace standing there. “I’m sorry, I…” She put her finger to his mouth.

“How long since Margaret?”

“Eight years.”

“Loneliness isn’t much fun, is it?” She looked over her shoulder. “One day those idiots will understand that.” Noel nodded sadly. “Anyway, how would you like to join me for dinner tomorrow night – at my house?”

“I’d love that.”

“Good, then. I’ll see you around about seven.”

Noel smiled and watched her walk back up the path. She stopped and turned back to look at him.

“And Noel.”

“Yeah.”

“Don’t wear that T-shirt. And don’t even think about calling me ‘doll’.”

He looked at her, unsure for a few seconds, then they both burst into fits of laughter. It seemed like it was going to be a good Christmas after all.

State of Self-Defence

He turned into Finnway Avenue. He couldn't see anything even resembling a dark transit van, and immediately felt some sort of relief. He was disturbed by a blue Suzuki Swift which turned in from Bell Street. As the car sped by him with a joyful indifference, his mind began to race. Perhaps it was all some sort of nightmare or hallucination. He had been under a lot of pressure recently. However, his momentary feeling of reprieve was shattered as, from the far end of this thoroughfare, a large, dark vehicle emerged quietly from its hiding place behind a parked furniture lorry. He was now more than three-quarters of the way down the long avenue, but could see that – despite a surprising lack of noise – the van was picking up speed. Halfway through a prayer, he stepped off the pavement and onto the road.

Peter Main studied the well-dressed but otherwise unremarkable man sitting on the other side of his Head Teacher's desk. "So, let me understand you. You are not the father of Peter Fraser? So…"

The stranger raised his right hand and spoke softly, “No, I’m not. Please forgive me, but…” Sensing an imminent protest from the Head, he raised his hand slightly higher, smiled and mouthed the word, “Please?”

Peter Main, who had begun to rise from his chair, sat back down and perched on the edge of his leather seat, still keeping his right hand over his desk phone.

“You’ve got ten seconds and then…”

“Please, Mr Main… anything else is unnecessary. I am here to show you something.” As he reached inside his thin, black briefcase, he saw Peter Main visibly stiffen. He smiled reassuringly at the Head Teacher as he pulled out an A4-sized manila envelope and laid it on the desk in front of him.

Feeling slightly less strained, Main instinctively moved his hand away from the telephone and settled back further into his chair. What the hell was going on? What on earth was the envelope about? The stranger seemed to read his thoughts and edged the envelope closer to him. “The answer is inside, Mr Main.”

A thousand thoughts raced through his mind: is this some sort of a ‘set-up’? Is someone threatening me? What am I committing to by opening this? Despite these feelings of dread, he tore open the envelope with his paper knife, paused for a few seconds and noted the unflinching eyes upon him. Gingerly holding the envelope in his left hand, he removed the single sheet of paper with his right thumb and forefinger. Staring at the single word on the sheet, he gently lowered the envelope onto his desk and set the paper on top of it. For what seemed to him like hours, but was probably just seconds, he was completely unaware of the stranger sitting opposite him. A sardonic grin appeared on his face now and he felt strangely relieved in that way that only knowledge can provide.

Now he laughed, slightly desperately. "I don't suppose there's any possibility of a mistake?"

The stranger was looking serious now, like a doctor sent to give bad news. "I'm afraid not, Sir. As you can see from the word on the sheet…"

Peter Main noticed the change in the personal address. It was funny, really. The pupils called him Sir every day, yet paradoxically it was one of the rare occasions when he wasn't transported back to another time and place. "My daughter's getting married next year," he said hesitatingly. "I suppose you'll point out that *they* missed out on things, too?" The stranger looked sympathetic, but said nothing. "I wondered about Jason when I saw that newspaper report."

"The hit and run, Sir?"

"Ha, ha. Yeah, the 'hit and run'. Is that what's in it for me? Is it?" The stranger shook his head dismissively. "Well, what the hell is it, then?"

The stranger looked serious, but spoke calmly and clearly, hesitating only when giving out vital place names or times. Tonight, Peter Main would go home to his family as normal; but then, around 9.35pm, he would discover he really needed cash for tomorrow. He would drive to a particular Cash Point and remove £80. Some time between collecting his money and returning to his car, Peter Main would be killed!

"I could refuse."

"You could, Sir. However, along with the others, you agreed – this way is best! Your family are best served financially by this outcome and… well, the trail will… disappear."

Main studied the man for a few seconds, then nodded. "I was just a boy myself really…"

"I don't judge you, Sir."

"No? It doesn't matter. Someone will – very shortly. What will he say?"

"That you were serving your country; that you were at war…"

"War? Can we call it that now? Yes, it was a war. Not that day, though. Christ, if it wasn't before, it certainly was afterwards. Did we… did I… cause even more deaths? Every time I went to the confessional… I saw them all…"

"A priest?" the stranger asked.

Lifting his eyes to meet the man's opposite, and seeing something unnervingly threatening, he immediately added, "Not the school Chaplain!"

The stranger smiled back reassuringly.

Main seemed to be staring at something far beyond the walls of his office. "The guy… 'my' guy…" He hesitated, then looked directly at the stranger. "He held his hands up. Like this." The Head Teacher realised that if anyone was to enter his office it would appear that he was surrendering to the man opposite him. Roles reversed. Lowering his hands, he whispered, "And I shot him."

The stranger rose slowly from his chair, then pushed it back to its original place against the wall. He made as if to leave by the door on his right-hand side, but then hesitated; he turned towards the desk again and picked up the manila envelope, before neatly tucking the paper with its single word – *January* – inside it. He almost spoke to Main, but the Head Teacher, now deep in thought, waved his hand dismissively in his direction. The stranger nodded, turned, opened the door and left.

Early Finish

What a beautiful, perfect day, he thought, as he looked out through the clear glass window which ran the full length of the room, towards the lush, green playing fields and beyond. There was a stillness, a calm. He loved mornings like this and wished that mornings had always been this way. A chance to relax, to feel good, before the inevitable tsunami of students engulfed his classroom on the second floor of St Jude High School. His gaze moved to the small, framed photograph on his desk and he smiled broadly. Life had never been…

Hearing the noise of a siren clamouring in the distance, again he looked beyond the school playing fields towards the road.

He didn't have long to wait before a police car came into view from his left-hand side. He tensed, but quickly reassured himself that at the end of that section of road there was a roundabout, hidden behind an office block and the local library, which offered vehicles a choice of three directions: only one doubled back towards the school. A loud wailing from his left distracted him from the original car's progress, and he saw two more police cars, flashing blue lights on top, come into view. As he turned to look back towards the road, the first police car could not be seen and he experienced difficulty locating the direction of its siren. As the two subsequent police cars were disappearing from view, simultaneously another appeared on his left. Then the first car pulled into the school playground, two floors below him.

He watched as the occupants of the first police car emerged from their vehicle and stood surveying the scene. He calmly backed away from the window. Quickly, he opened his bottom left-hand desk drawer and, from a narrow, flat box took out a Stanley knife, its shiny blade fixed and uncovered. He moved the desk away from him, dropped to his knees and ran the blade around two of the carpet squares located under the two right legs of the table.

Ignoring the crescendo which was rapidly building from the sirens below his window, he cut around the flooring underneath. It lifted easily and he pulled from the hole a black holdall. Laying it behind him, he proceeded to quickly, but carefully, replace the flooring and the carpet tiles and the desk to their original places. He stood up and unzipped the bag. He quickly checked that everything was in order: the three passports, the currency, the credit cards, the gun.

Satisfied, he took out the gun, placing it in his trouser belt underneath his sleeveless jumper, before re-zipping the bag. He surveyed the scene outside. There were now – as far as he could make out – three marked police cars in the playground. Two other cars were parked alongside them, so he assumed that they must also have brought more police to the party! He also noted that police cars were now in position at either end of the road beyond the fields – keeping back anyone overly inquisitive or just plain stupid!

"Have you seen…?"

Momentarily startled, his hand immediately shot towards his belt, but rested there. He looked at the tall, slim, blonde female who had just entered. He sighed and smiled at her. She immediately understood that he was relieved, but understood also that the warmth of the smile was genuine. She started to speak, but his voice cut across hers.

"We need to leave. We need to leave now." Again she started to speak; again he spoke over her. "You love me? You trust me? We need to leave – now."

"I don't understand. What's goi..."

"You believe I love you?"

She nodded.

"Good. Let's go." He grabbed her hand and led her towards the classroom door. She pulled her hand free.

"What if I hadn't come in? Would you have just disappeared?"

He tried his best reassuring smile, but could see it wasn't going to be enough. Looking directly at her, he carefully placed the holdall on one of the student school desks. Pulling back the zip, he took out one of the three passports and handed it to her. She opened it and there was her photograph – not a name she recognised – but certainly her photograph. Before she could say anything, he took the passport from her, placed it inside and re-zipped the holdall. "You were always coming."

His eyes told her that the talking was over and she allowed him to lead her outside the classroom, half-way along the long corridor, before turning right and heading out through a set of doors which led to the stairway which ran just inside the outer wall. The noise from the police sirens grew louder as they descended. At the first floor, he signalled for her to stop and wait while he pulled back one of the two double doors and went out onto the lower corridor. On this floor he had a clear view of the ground level and quickly noted that there were now a fair number of students gathered in pockets of various sizes, but it didn't look like many had ventured outside to greet the sizeable police presence.

From further down the corridor, Thomas Flynn emerged from his classroom and looked over the railings to the ground floor. He turned, and, spotting his colleague, gave him a little shrug, as if seeking an explanation. Noting the shake of the head, he acknowledged and went back into the classroom.

Just as he turned towards the stairway, he noticed that uniformed policemen – a half dozen or so – were starting to emerge through the front entrance to the hall. Without moving his eyes from the scene below, he took three steps backward and brought his elbow crashing into the fire alarm button.

United, they sped down the one flight of stairs and moved into the main hall. All students were now congregated around the front door or one of the two fire exits which were positioned near the centre of the wall opposite and around six metres to the left of the doors from which they had just emerged. Without breaking stride, he led her to their right and to her own classroom, which she had left only minutes ago. Having closed the door from the inside, he made his way to the back left-hand side of the room and began to pull the rectangular table and two chairs behind it away from a wall door.

"That's locked."

Without turning, he took out a single key, placed it in the lock and turned it easily. He motioned for her to follow him. There was a drop of about three feet into a basement which seemed to be populated by an assortment of broken desks and chairs and an old set of five-a-side goalposts. He jumped down, spun around and offered his hand to help her down. She hesitated.

"I need to get my phone. It's in my desk."

"No. No phone." He noticed in her a hesitation. They stared at each other for what seemed like light years, but were in actuality just seconds.

"My photos… I need to get my photos… of my mum."

He nodded. "Okay. Toss me down your bag."

She stopped. Everything had been such a whirl from that moment when she had walked into his classroom to find out if he knew anything about the commotion outside; it seemed as if she had forgotten that she had been carrying a small handbag. She handed it to him and, as he threw the long strap from it around his neck, he began to clear some of the 'furniture' to one side. She had immediately gone back into the classroom and he could hear her rummaging through her desk drawers as, from her bag, he detected a faint vibration.

He heard her draw the student desk back into position, before positioning herself on the narrow ledge on the inside and drawing the door closed behind her. She saw that he had left the keys in the storeroom side of the door, so she quickly turned the lock and hopped onto the cold grey floor. By now he was standing on the opposite side of the small room. Around knee height down to the floor, she noticed there was a hole in the wall. He beckoned her towards him and when he saw she was approaching, he got down on his knees, then backed into the space behind him.

She backed in the same way and discovered another drop. Longer this time. As he lifted a perfectly cut piece of plasterboard into the space they had just crawled through, she took in the scene around her. She could still hear the police sirens and now, through gaps in the wooden surround, she could see the tyres and chassis of the various cars in the playground: they were underneath the school.

He was by her side again as he pointed to the far side of the building. Sensing he was about to lead them into a sprint, she stopped. "My bag!" He handed it to her without hesitation and guided her forward. Upon reaching the far end, he carefully eased four planks of wood away from the rest of the surround. Seeing how easily they had come away in his hands, she realised that this route had been well planned. "There's a car parked on the other side of Tesco, in Chalmers Court. We'll be there in two minutes. Let's go!"

"You first."

Throwing his holdall onto the grass outside, he quickly followed it through the gap. As he bent forward to pick it up, with his back to the building, he heard the unmistakeable sound of a revolver's hammer being cocked.

Aware that the noise had come from the gap in the wooden fencing that he had just left, he stood up slowly, but seemed to rule out turning around. The next noise he heard was the sound of the trigger being primed.

Click.

Then again: click, click.

Now he turned to face her. She was pointing the gun at his chest, but she looked confused – and frightened. She pulled the trigger rapidly.

Click.

Click.

Click.

She stood wide-eyed and open-mouthed. For a few seconds their eyes locked. Then he opened his right hand, containing six unused bullets.

"Sir?"

He looked to his left and immediately recognised a Year 3 student of his: Kevin Sprake.

"What a mess, eh? That clown Mr Greig has been drinking again. Phoned the cops and said that he was about to blow up the school. Told them to come and get him. My big brother found him semi-conscious in his class… phoned me before I got inside the gate. I'm going for a coffee before I head in. It's crazy in there."

He smiled and nodded at Kevin, who was blissfully unaware of the third figure hidden from view, who had dropped both her hands to her side. Turning towards the gap, he again stared into the darkness and said quietly, "I guess we'd better get back to school. That's enough excitement for one day."

www.ingramcontent.com/pod-product-compliance
Ingram Content Group UK Ltd.
Pitfield, Milton Keynes, MK11 3LW, UK
UKHW040003200726
13854UKWH00001B/22

9 781784 658014